PARENTS AND CAREGIVERS,

Stone Arch Readers are designed to provide enjoyable reading experiences, as well as opportunities to develop vocabulary, literacy skills, and comprehension. Here are a few ways to support your beginning reader:

- Talk with your child about the ideas addressed in the story.

- Discuss each illustration, mentioning the characters, where they are, and what they are doing.

- Read with expression, pointing to each word. You may want to read the whole story through and then revisit parts of the story to ensure that the meanings of words or phrases are understood.

- Talk about why the character did what he or she did and what your child would do in that situation.

- Help your child connect with characters and events in the story.

Remember, reading with your child should be fun, not forced. Each moment spent reading with your child is a priceless investment in his or her literacy life.

GAIL SAUNDERS-SMITH, PH.D.

STONE ARCH READERS

are published by Stone Arch Books
151 Good Counsel Drive, P.O. Box 669
Mankato, Minnesota 56002
www.stonearchbooks.com

Library of Congress
Cataloging-in-Publication Data
Meister, Cari.
  Ora, the sea monster / by Cari Meister;
illustrated by Dennis Messner.
    p. cm. – (Stone Arch readers)
  ISBN 978-1-4342-1631-1 (library binding)
  ISBN 978-1-4342-1746-2 (paperback)
  [1. Gold–Fiction. 2. Sea monsters–Fiction.]
I. Messner, Dennis, ill. II. Title.
  PZ7.M515916Orb 2010
  [E]–dc22   2009000888

Summary: To earn gold, Ora helps a boy stop a giant.

Creative Director: Heather Kindseth
Designer: Bob Lentz

Reading Consultants:
Gail Saunders-Smith, Ph.D.
Melinda Melton Crow, M.Ed.
Laurie K. Holland, Media Specialist

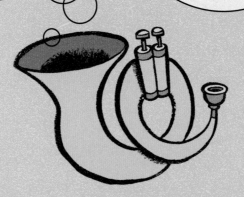

Printed in the United States of America

ORA

THE SEA MONSTER

BY CARI MEISTER

ILLUSTRATED BY
DENNIS MESSNER

STONE ARCH BOOKS
MINNEAPOLIS   SAN DIEGO

ORA

This is Ora. She has two wings. She has four arms.

Ora has six toes on each foot.

Ora likes gold. She has gold coins. She has gold pots. She even has a gold cat.

Ora hides her treasure in the deep sea.

Ora lives under the water. She comes out for one thing.

She comes out to look for
more gold.

It is early in the morning. Ora is looking for gold.

Ora digs in the sand. No gold.

She looks by a tree. No gold.

Ora looks in a cave. No gold.

She sees a boy in the cave.

"Can you help me?" asks the
boy. "A giant is at my castle.
Can you stop him?"

Ora does not know what
to say. She has never helped
anyone before.

Ora shakes her empty purse.
She points to her toes.

"I see," says the boy. "You want gold." Ora nods. The boy runs out of the cave.

The boy comes back. He has
a gold horn. "It makes music,"
he says.

Ora claps her hands. She likes
music.

"If you make the giant go away, you can have the horn," says the boy.

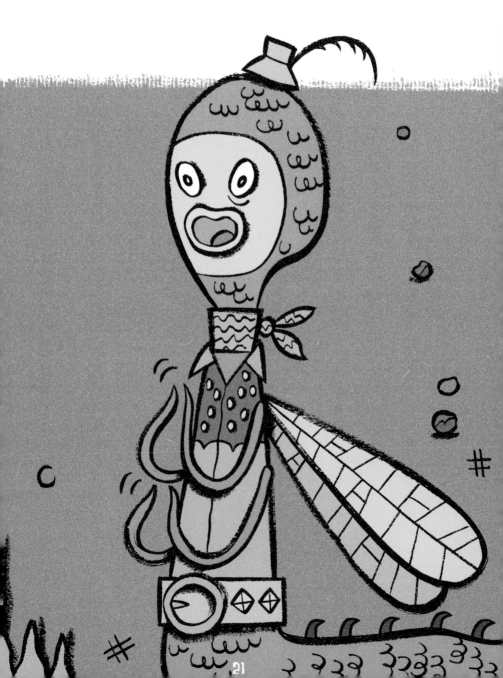

Ora flies to the boy's castle.
She sees the giant.

"Ha, ha, ha!" the giant laughs.
He throws a big rock at Ora.

Ora roars. She moves to the ground so the big rock will not hit her.

The giant laughs. He jumps
up and down. He thinks that he
has hit Ora.

"I win! I win!" the giant says.

Now Ora is really mad. She
blows flames.

"Oh no! My pants are on fire," says the giant. "My mother made these for me. I am going to be in big trouble!"

The giant runs away.

"Thank you," says the boy.
"You saved my castle."

He gives Ora the gold horn.

Ora goes back to the sea.

She loves her new treasure.

THE END

STORY WORDS

treasure   empty

giant   ground

castle

Total Word Count: 316

MEET ALL FOUR OF OUR MONSTERS!